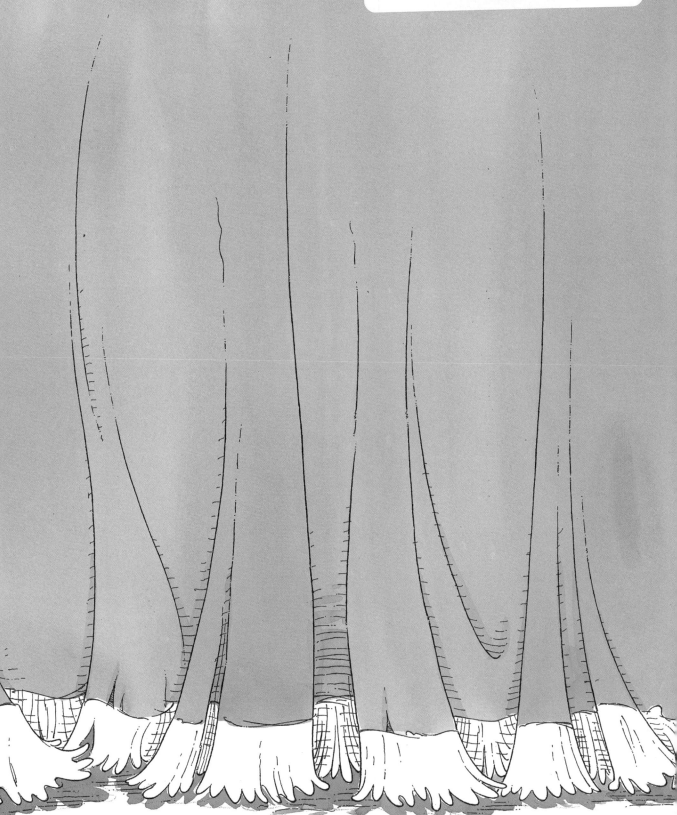

Script by
J. DAVID STEM
&
DAVID N. WEISS

Illustrated
by
TED ENIK

KAY THOMPSON'S
ELOISE
IN
HOLLYWOOD

BASED ON THE ART OF
HILARY KNIGHT

Simon & Schuster Books for Young Readers

NEW YORK · LONDON · TORONTO · SYDNEY

SIMON & SCHUSTER BOOKS FOR YOUNG READERS

An imprint of Simon & Schuster Children's Publishing Division

1230 Avenue of the Americas, New York, New York 10020

Text copyright © 2007 by the Estate of Kay Thompson

Illustrations by Hilary Knight and Ted Enik copyright © 2007 by the Estate of Kay Thompson

All rights reserved, including the right of reproduction in whole or in part in any form.

SIMON & SCHUSTER BOOKS FOR YOUNG READERS is a trademark of Simon & Schuster, Inc.

"Eloise" and related marks are trademarks of the Estate of Kay Thompson.

Book design by Marc Cheshire

Art colored by Joe Ewers

The text for this book is set in ITC Bodoni Seventy-Two.

The illustrations for this book are rendered in pen-and-ink and watercolor.

Manufactured in the United States of America

2 4 6 8 10 9 7 5 3 1

CIP data for this book is available from the Library of Congress.

ISBN-13: 978-0-689-84289-4

ISBN-10: 0-689-84289-9

There was this one time
when Weenie and I were
teaching Skipperdee
how to make a proper landing
behind enemy lines

Because they never expect you
to send a turtle

And this phone was ringing practically right off the hook
But thankfully it was my mother calling
to speak with Nanny and she had the
most absolutely fabulous news
See here's the thing of it

If your mother is even one-half worth her salt
then sooner or later
she's bound to make the acquaintance of
a famous Hollywood Movie Mogul
who will insist you simply
must must must
drop in for a visit

The first thing you have to do if you're going to Hollywood California is start packing

You have to be careful what you take
when you venture out to Hollywood
because there's this weather there
that is absolutely goooooorgeous

so you'll need all these sundries
for the surf and the pool
and for generally lying about
which is what they do in Hollywood
all year round for Lord's sake

so you simply must have
at least three pairs of sunglasses
or you'll be stuck with the same old peepers
for brunch, sporting events,
and evening rendezvouses
wherein everyone who's anyone
absolutely insists on going
in . . . cog . . . nito

Be sure to pack extra
for the children

You'll need to hobnob on the set
Catch a premiere

Take lunch all over town
And see and be seen with
everyone who's anyone at all

I'm a big fan of the cinema
Here's how many movie premieres
my mother has attended: 6
Here's how many movies I've been in: 0

Here's what to do if your public
lines up to see you off
Wave a tearful good-bye and
blow all these kisses
with *both* of your hands

Even Mr. Salomone couldn't resist
catching a glimpse as we were
whisked to our carriage

We informed him
we might not return
for several weeks

He took it *rawther* well

Even though there are all these airplanes that flit about from here to there
on a regular basis here's what many famous studio types will only go by

TRAIN!

Nanny says the one thing
you absolutely must do on a train
is eat eat eat

There's a whole car just for it but you have to bring your own raisins and roast-beef bone and Room Service
But you can still say "Charge it please . . . to me ELOISE"

When
traveling by rail
always keep an eye out
for these great train
robbers or these
angry Indians

Mostly trains
are *filled* with spies
But they never tell
you that

My mother's Mogul sent his Mercedes
and his driver Monty to meet us

Absolutely everything a Mogul owns is monogrammed with an M
Marvelous!
Monty talks just like Nanny
and guessed what village
in jolly old England she was from

It sounded like steak sauce

One place everyone wants to live in Hollywood is the Hills
Here's what Beverly Hills is
Flat

There are all these maps on the corner
so you can find everyone and take their picture

On the way to our hotel Monty thought we might enjoy some sightseeing
if only all these *daft ninnies* would learn to drive
Nanny said "Well I never ever ever"
and we got out and walked

There are all kinds of stars in Hollywood
If you are good the Mayor will give you
a star of your own on the sidewalk
(which is rawther filthy I must say)

Nanny says lots of people in Hollywood are lost lost lost
I guess that's why they have a sign
telling them where they are

The Hollywood Sign

Hollywood Boulevard

Walk of Stars

Schwab's!

The Capitol Records Bldg.

Venice Beach

But there's absolutely no one forgetting *who* they are in Hollywood
because they plunk you down in your good shoes in the wet cement
and have you write your name which is quite frowned upon at The Plaza
but as they say in Hollywood

Anything Goes

Three good things
about the
Hollywood
Hills
Hotel

It's
PINK
PINK
PINK

The Concierge is *very* friendly with my mother's Mogul
Here's what he likes to say
"Enjoy, Dahlings! Why shouldn't you?"
Everyone in Hollywood is *DAHLING*!

Nanny Dahling says there is absolutely nothing
like a long hot bawth bawth bawth
after a frightful train ride
to ease your rheumatism

Cocktails are served in the Jockey Club promptly at 7

Shirley Temple is a Movie Star *and* a cocktail
Ditto Roy Rogers
When Nanny burps she says "God save the Queen"
When I burp I say "More please!"

The Jockey Club is the ONLY place
in this town to make a deal and drink gin
Here's how to make a deal
Have your people call my people
and then get back to their people

Lots of agents are on all these phones
making all these deals
so everyone talks with their mouth full

The Concierge spoke
to the Maitre d' in Spanish
and got us a table on the double
where Humphrey Bogart used to sit
I spoke Spanish to the waiter
and got uno raisin,
dos roast-beef bones,
and cuatro spoons pronto

And everyone was saying "Good night Dahling"
and "Kiss kiss" and there are all these coyotes
which are absolutely not allowed at The Plaza
singing Ooooooooooooooooooo
out there in the dark somewhere

We skibbled off to bed
in our robes with HHH on the pocket
and our HHH slippers with HHH on the toes
what else?

Here's what you have to look out for in Hollywood
An Earthquake

Breakfast is always served poolside in Hollywood but there's very little coffee only all these Moguls asking for espresso and cappuccino and half-caf and latte and Nanny Dahling wondering what would the Queen say?

Here's what you read with your berries if you're from Hollywood:
Variety
Here's what you're in if you read *Variety*: "The Business"

One thing to remember when you are out yachting in Hollywood
Avoid having any really good sea battles
if you see this really spoiled-looking boy
with his sunglasses on
and all these people treating him like
he's the crown prince of Brunei

After breakfast Monty rang and said we had to get the show on the road PRONTO . . .
so you can imagine
Here's what everyone loves in Hollywood
Their car

In the back of a Mercedes there are all these buttons for pushing
but there's hardly time to push them all unless you push them very fast
or all at once and then the windows are practically going out of their mind
with all this buzzing and the lights are all flickery but your botto's
absolutely warm and cozy for a change so that's good

You have to be on The List to visit Hollywood
They always say "Name please"
And I just say it's me ELOISE!

We met this girl
at the studio named Ida
She's the Mogul's gopher
but doesn't look like one
Ida went to Radcliffe
where they taught her how to
make coffee and GO FOR things

KEEP OUT!
This Means
YOU
MAMMOTH MOVI
MESSENGER
WHERE THE WIND WENT
SCRIPTS

Ida is 27 and always carries licorice and loves to tap dance in the elevator
But what she really wants to do is direct

She directed us to the line for people
who are waiting to be discovered
Of course I don't have to be discovered
because I'm me ELOISE

My mother's Mogul already told the director to cast me in his latest epic

So we cut in front

We had to wait
to see the director . . .
and wait . . .
and wait . . .

so I read the script for the epic
It's all about this brave little boy who saves his town
from this *rawther* large sort of ape
who was smashing all of these buildings
into very small pieces and stomping around
without looking where he was going at all

The brave kid saves the day
in this old airplane

Diego is my director
He's from Venezuela and smells like coffee and Cuban cigars

I showed him I can act by sklathing about like I have gout
And lolling this way and that with dysentery I got fighting this alligator

And sklanking from here to there with an arrow sticking out of my side
from that time I was ambushed in Transylvania by a Vampire . . .

. . . and these Wolves and a fuzzy Caterpillar
   when they got the jump on me
   because I had captured their old friend the Mummy

Here's the thing about acting

You have to be able to improvise

Diego said "Vamos! Vamos!"
which is "Let's go!"
And "No más" which is español
for "No worries"

He was very impressed

Of course if you are going to be in a film
you simply must go to wardrobe and be fitted

And then of course
there's makeup

A movie set is the most exciting place in the world

For the first two minutes

RESERVED FOR
★ STAR! ★

They don't tell you this
when you buy your pop-pop-popcorn

but making a movie is mostly waiting . . .

waiting . . .

waitinggggggggg

Finally the star arrived
and we could all hop to it.
His name is Corky Durbin
and he's hot hot hot
after doing that picture
where he plays the boy genius
who solves crimes for the President

Apparently it's a crime to sit in his chair

Mr. Diego spent a lot of time yelling "ACTION"
and "CUT CUT CUT"
and "Una más! Con ánimo!"

My botto got very fidgety so Ida gave me some licorice
which she will give you if you show her you know how to play the quiet game

She will also give it to you
if you show her you know how to play
the LOUD game

And then you have to wait some more
and then before you know it
it's time for your close-up
with Mr. DeMille

And then it's back to all this waiting again
while they get the giant ape
to do all this stomping in just the right place

Or they have to try it una más again
only this time con more ánimo.

After more waiting and close-ups
and waiting and fade-outs
we went to the screening room
to watch the "dailies"

Even though it was night

The first thing you have to do at dailies is say "Roll 'em"

After watching the ape bashing and planes crashing
and lots of Corky Corky Corky
there was me ELOISE in my screen debut

It helps if you stand closer

I must admit I was really marvelous
Nanny says I will be a great star
and that next time I'll have a better picture

Skipperdee and Weenie thought I was marvelous too

There's not much more to say about Hollywood Dahling

Just more of parties

And doing lunch

And 2 o'clocks and 5 o'clocks

And more dailies

And more cars

And then it's good-bye Dahling, kiss kiss, and cheerio!

So when all of these fans ask me whatever I think about acting in Hollywood California

I absolutely pretty much recommend it a lot

Because an actor's life can be *most* rewarding

Especially if you always remember to never forget the little people who knew you when

So Dahling

as we say in Hollywood

Break your leg

That means "good luck"

Of course

what I *really* want to do is direct